For my sisters and the
sunshine they bring.

H.E.

For my brother, who has taken care
of me since we were little and still
does, though from a distance.

A.L.

First American Edition 2020
Kane Miller, A Division of EDC Publishing
www.kanemiller.com
First published in Great-Britain 2020 by Caterpillar Books Ltd,
an imprint of the Little Tiger Group
Text by Harriet Evans
Text copyright © Caterpillar Books Ltd 2020
Illustrations copyright © Andrés Landazábal 2020

Library of Congress Control Number: 2019941884
Printed in China
ISBN: 978-1-68464-052-2
CPB/1400/1343/1219
13 5 7 9 10 8 6 4 2

A Celebration
of
Sisters

Sisters share all your hopes,

and they soothe all your fears,

as days drift to months,

and float into years.

Your life twists and it turns,
leaps up and sinks down,

but sisters stay constant
and smooth out your frown.

You'll wait and you'll wonder
who your sister will be,

and though you may worry,

she'll be great – wait and see!

Older sisters might lead,
or take a back seat,

for each bold adventure
and daring new feat.

Little sisters may copy

your style and your walk.

You'll be their first choice
when they need to talk.

Friends can become sisters
as you grow up together,

facing dark storms
and enjoying fair weather.

Sisters may irritate

and sometimes they're rude,

but on your worst days
they'll brighten your mood.

Mess somehow just happens
as you both start to scheme,

but it turns out all right
when you work as a team.

Adventures are better
with a sister or two,

through thick and through thin,
you make a great crew!

Sisters share all your hopes,

and they soothe all your fears,

as days drift to months ...

... and float into years.